"I thoroughly enjoyed getting to know Linda Taylor's colorful character of *Amazing Annabelle*. She is confident, charming, gutsy, and smart. She is a go-getter who does not let anything or anyone keep her down. I can hardly wait to follow Annabelle in her other adventures."

—*Paulette Williams, Assistant Principal*

"Amazing Annabelle is truly an amazing character! She possesses personality traits that we can all strive for: self-confidence, perseverance, compassion, endurance, and problem solving. She has such a wonderful outlook on life and finds the positive in any situation. What a great role model!

"This is a great character education story that can be read across the elementary grade levels. While reading the story, I was able to bring Annabelle to life in my mind. The illustrations are fabulous! I look forward to reading all her adventures. Such a wonderful gift of storytelling. Well done!"

—*Pam Doughty, Teacher*

"I loved Linda Taylor's character development. There were many times in the story when I thought the author must have been a fly on the wall in my house. I thought the characters were very real and diverse. I think she has come up with a great idea for a children's book series!"

—*Jennifer Hall, Parent*

Amazing Annabelle

DECEMBER HOLIDAYS AND CELEBRATIONS

LINDA TAYLOR

ILLUSTRATED BY KYLE HORNE

Lightswitch
LEARNING
a Sussman Education company

250 East 54th Street, P2
New York, NY 10022

www.lightswitchlearning.com

Educators and Librarians, for a variety of teaching resources, visit
www.lightswitchlearning.com

ISBN: 978-1-94782903-9

Printed in China

To my countless

students—

Oh, how you've

inspired me!

Contents

December Holidays
and Celebrations

December is a festive month.
I'm sure you would agree.
Hanukkah, Christmas, and Kwanzaa
Annabelle encounters all three.

Embracing many cultures
With a Super Holiday Celebration.
Melville Elementary School
Has really high expectations.

1

HANUKKAH LESSONS

December is always a festive time of the year, especially for Annabelle and her family. There are so many activities, parties, celebrations, and presents during the holidays. Annabelle always connected with the joys of the season and became involved in many beneficial projects.

One thing Annabelle and her family loved to do each year was volunteer at the Children's Hope Charity that raised money for needy children and their families. In December they bought presents with all the money that was donated throughout the year.

The charity also hosted a big holiday party for all the kids every year, and Santa came and passed out toys to everyone. Annabelle always loved to dress up as an elf and helped Santa.

She really enjoyed playing games with the kids and seeing the smiles on all their happy faces. This was just one of the activities that was near and dear to Annabelle's heart.

A lot was happening at Melville School during December as well. The entire school recognized all three December holidays: Hanukkah, Christmas, and Kwanzaa. Highlighting the value of each was important.

In Mrs. Mitchell's class, they were going to have mini-activities, arts and crafts, and celebrations for each individual holiday. And then the whole school planned to have a great big

Holiday Bash, a fun evening in a setting like a carnival.

Just the mention of this Holiday Bash made Annabelle's eyes become wide with wonder and surprise. During this time of the year, everyone was buzzing with talk of topping last year's Holiday Bash. Annabelle was already thinking about some ideas in that amazing mind of hers.

On the first day of December, Mrs. Mitchell read the class a story about Hanukkah. What made the lesson so great was that afterwards, she let Caleb and Julia share their personal Hanukkah experiences with the whole class.

Caleb talked about lighting one of the eight candles on the menorah each night using the Shamash candle, which is the helper candle centered in the middle of the menorah. He also said his favorite Hanukkah meal was brisket and potato latkes, which is similar to a potato pancake.

Julia told the class that her family always played the dreidel game in the living room after dinner. She also shared how her grandpa always gave all the kids in the house Hanukkah gelt, which are chocolate coins, after they play the game.

Annabelle learned more about Hanukkah from listening to Caleb and Julia's stories than she did listening to Mrs. Mitchell read the book about it! Annabelle raised her hand to ask a question.

"Mrs. Mitchell, do you think it would be a good idea to actually taste some of the foods Caleb talked about?" she asked.

The entire class liked her idea and thought they should do it.

"That certainly would be a tasty idea, but I don't know who would volunteer to make everything for our class," Mrs. Mitchell said.

Caleb immediately raised his hand and said, "I'm sure my mom wouldn't mind making some latkes for the whole class. I'll ask her when I get home."

"Maybe I could bring in some Hanukkah gelt for the class to try also," Julia added.

The class was really excited over the fact that they might get to taste some new holiday treats. That would be an opportunity for real authentic learning, as Mrs. Mitchell would say.

Mrs. Mitchell always tried to give her class real experiences that brought the learning topic to life. That is just one of the many reasons why Annabelle loved being in her class.

The next day at school, Caleb brought in a big platter of latkes and Julia brought in a big bag of Hanukkah gelt! She also brought in a box of dreidels so she could teach the class how to play the game.

Everyone was excited except Barry. He started to make a very ugly face. He was a very picky eater who barely ate his own lunch each day in the cafeteria. Barry was getting sick just thinking about eating the latkes and gelt. Mrs. Mitchell noticed the strange look on his face.

"Barry, how are you feeling? You really don't look well. Do you need to go to the nurse or something?" Mrs. Mitchell asked as she felt his forehead.

"You don't feel warm or anything. How are you feeling?" she asked again.

Barry finally spoke up. "I'm not really a big fan of foods from other places, Mrs. Mitchell. If it's all the same to you, I'd rather not have any of the Hanukkah foods today." At least Barry was respectful.

"Of course, Barry, I completely understand. And if anyone doesn't like the taste of a latke, you certainly don't have to eat it. We really just wanted you to experience the holiday a little through food," Mrs. Mitchell explained.

Mrs. Mitchell divided up the latkes and gave them to the students to taste. The majority of the class liked it and ate the whole pancake. Some just tasted a little and threw the rest away. Caleb's mom had typed the recipe out and had made copies for all the students to take home.

After everyone was finished eating, Julia explained how to play the dreidel game. She brought in four dreidels to share with everyone.

Mrs. Mitchell divided the class into four groups and gave each group gelt, which are chocolate coins, to put into a large bowl that was a part of the game. Each group member took turns spinning the dreidel as they played. By the end of class, everyone had become an expert at playing the game.

2

HOLIDAY BASH COMMITTEE

Annabelle and Kaitlyn were both on the same committee together, which to their enjoyment, had happened before. This time it was the Holiday Bash Committee. They both offered to join the committee because not many students were signing up for it. Everyone knew it was time-consuming and would include much detailed work.

Around this holiday season, people were already busy enough with many other fun activities. Annabelle's dad always told her that life can get very hectic quickly if you don't pace yourself and take it one day at a time. And that is exactly what Annabelle always did.

Annabelle always loved projects like this. It allowed her to put her creative juices to work in a positive way. Kaitlyn loved parties and excitement, which is great.

However, Annabelle wanted to be thoroughly involved in making dreams come true for others and putting smiles on their faces. She also understood how much hard work it took to accomplish these goals. She enjoyed putting things together that people would not soon forget. Annabelle's dad would always say she was a pioneer ahead of her time.

After school, the Holiday Bash Committee met in Mrs. Kessler's room. She was a fourth-grade teacher at Melville School and was known for being strict and very serious. Annabelle had never met her before, but the whole school knew of her ways. Annabelle wondered how on earth she was placed in charge of such an important fun event, taking into consideration her well-known personality.

Only four students attended the meeting, including Annabelle, Kaitlyn, Adele, and Barry. Barry, being the only guy, felt a little out of place, but he still stayed because his friends were there. Two P.T.A. moms showed up as well— Mrs. Stewart and Mrs. Jacobson. Mrs. Kessler, of course, was also there, and she didn't seem happy at all.

Mrs. Jacobson, who was actually the P.T.A. president, started the meeting discussion. "As you know, the school wants to host a spectacular Holiday Bash this year, and we're looking to see how we can make it even better than last year," Mrs. Jacobson began. "I want to open up our meeting by everyone sharing any grand ideas you may have."

Mrs. Kessler was the first to share her opinion. "Well," she said, "I think it's a good idea to just do the same thing we did last year. Everyone loved it. So why do we have to reinvent the wheel?" There was no excitement at all in Mrs. Kessler's voice.

Mrs. Jacobson looked at Mrs. Kessler as if she had two heads on her body.

"That would defeat the whole purpose of coming up with something new and equally as exciting as last year, Mrs. Kessler," said Mrs. Jacobson. "Everyone loves something that they haven't experienced before and are just seeing for the first time. That's what we're trying to capture here for our Holiday Bash."

Mrs. Stewart, the other P.T.A. parent, agreed.

"Just imagine having a fresh take or a different angle on the holidays this year. I'm looking for something current and inspiring," Mrs. Stewart said.

Mrs. Kessler let out a long sigh and shook her head. It was very obvious that she was definitely *not* on the same page as the P.T.A. moms.

With the way they both spoke, Mrs. Kessler was thinking they were trying to put together some kind of show-stopping Broadway-bound Superstar Holiday Extravaganza! Mrs. Kessler didn't think Melville School was ready for all that drama.

Annabelle sensed an uncomfortable tone and a difference in the general ideas being brought up in the meeting by the adults. She thought this would be a good time to share her own plans.

"I have a great idea that we could have

three different stations—a Hanukkah station, a Christmas station, and a Kwanzaa station. In each station, we could have special crafts and games. Once you visit each station and do the activities, you'll get a special ticket to enter the Winter Wonderland area," Annabelle said.

"I love it, I love it, I love it! That has never been done before!" Mrs. Jacobson said excitedly.

"I think you are on to something big, Annabelle. Go on, what's going to happen next?" Mrs. Stewart asked.

"When they get to the Winter Wonderland area, they can make edible snowmen and decorate holiday cookies and all sorts of treats there," Annabelle explained.

"They can also join a super dance party with a DJ playing some holiday songs!" Kaitlyn said, remembering how much the students loved the dance booth at the Apple Celebration.

The P.T.A. moms and the other students had smiles of approval on their faces. But everyone noticed that Mrs. Kessler had a worried look on her face.

"That might be too much, girls," she warned. "You're talking about two different things happening in two different places!"

Adele, one of the other students, came up with a great answer to this concern. "Exactly. We could have the stations in the auditorium, and then we could set up the Winter Wonderland in the gymnasium!" Adele said.

Out of nowhere, with a burst of enthusiasm, Barry shouted, "Wahoo! That sounds awesome!"

Everyone laughed except Mrs. Kessler, who put a cloud on the moment.

"I still think we may have to reconsider parts of this big idea and scale it down a little," Mrs. Kessler said.

"Actually, I think it's perfect just the way it is!" Mrs. Jacobson announced.

All the students nodded their heads

and made positive remarks in agreement with Mrs. Jacobson.

"This is just the kind of interesting experience we need here at Melville School!" Mrs. Stewart said.

"Not only is the idea exciting, it's also going to supply all the students with a learning experience about other cultures and holiday practices!" Mrs. Jacobson exclaimed.

It seems as if Mrs. Kessler was outvoted on all sides of her argument. She finally concluded that if you can't beat them, then you must join them.

"I guess we can try this plan and see what happens," said Mrs. Kessler.

"All right! Let's get this party started!" Barry added and everyone started laughing again.

3

CHRISTMAS TREE SHOPPING

Annabelle was excited for Saturday to come, and finally it was here! Her family always put up their Christmas tree and decorations on the first Saturday in December. Dad, Mom, Annabelle, her little brother, Jason, and even her big sister, Alice, all went to the Christmas tree lot to pick the best tree for their house. As soon as they arrived, Jason immediately went running to what he thought was the best Christmas tree ever.

"Hey, everyone, I found it," he yelled, thrilled at his choice. This is the one; I just know it! Let's put it on top of the car right now."

No one else seemed to be convinced about Jason's choice.

"Listen, Big Head," said Alice, "we just got here. We need time to look around at all the trees before we just go rushing to pick the first one in sight."

"Now, don't call your brother Big Head, Alice," corrected Dad. "But Jason, she does have a point. Let's take a little more time to walk around and search down all the rows instead of just settling on the first one we see, okay buddy?"

"I guess so," answered Jason disappointed. "But there are so many trees! We could be here forever!"

"You have to be patient, Jason," said Mom. "Don't worry, we'll find just the right one."

Annabelle had gone on her own search for the perfect tree, and she had done her homework.

"Hey, everyone, come down here!" Annabelle called out to her family from the end of the row.

Everyone walked down to where Annabelle was standing.

"So what are we looking at here, Annabelle?" Dad asked, wondering if his daughter knew anything about the tree.

"This is a beautiful white spruce, Dad!" said Annabelle. "It's a very popular tree. It has a great shape, a great smell, and the needles don't fall off easily." Annabelle sounded like a salesperson as she described the tree to her family.

"It seems as though you've really done a lot of research on the trees this year, Annabelle," Mom said, sounding impressed.

Alice walked to another tree standing three trees away.

"I like this one instead," she said. "It's so much taller!"

As everyone went over to look at it, Annabelle was thinking that she knew a little something about this tree as well.

"Now this one is a scotch pine; it's also a very good tree. It's easy to replant and the needles stay on too. Either one would be a great choice," Annabelle decided.

"Why don't we just do 'eeny-meeny-miney-moe' and choose a tree already? I'm getting tired," Jason said in a cranky voice.

"Okay, let's take a vote. All in favor of the white spruce, raise your hand," Dad said.

Annabelle, Mom, and Jason raised their hand. Since there were only two people left to vote, the white spruce won.

But as Annabelle looked at Alice's sad face, she immediately took her hand down and changed her mind.

"You know, I think I want the scotch pine instead. It *is* a lot bigger," Annabelle declared.

"The bigger the better, little sis!" Alice said with a big smile on her face.

Annabelle hoped Alice was just talking about the tree and not herself being the oldest child.

"So, the scotch pine it is! Let's go pay for this tree and get it on top of the car," Dad said.

Jason jumped up and down. "Yes! Finally! Now we can go!"

"I'll meet you at the register in a little while. I just want to pick up a wreath and some garland for decoration in their store," Mom told her husband and ran off quickly.

Annabelle didn't mind giving in to Alice because she knew it really didn't matter one way or the other. She knew that Christmas was not about getting your own way or proving how much you know about something. Besides, this day was a great family outing, and Annabelle wasn't about to ruin it for anything. Her mom had told her it's always better to keep the peace than to cause a battle in some situations.

As they headed home, Annabelle realized that Alice was speaking in a sweeter way than usual and carrying on a pleasant conversation with her. This really didn't happen that often.

Most of the time, Alice was in her own little world. Alice would say a few words to Annabelle from time to time, but nothing too serious or long.

Annabelle had always looked up to Alice, but she also realized that Alice could be a little pushy and picky at times. She just thought that big sisters can be that way at times once they reach a certain age.

So, Annabelle really appreciated this

time in the car to bond with her sister. She didn't know how long it would last, but Annabelle was just going to enjoy the moment.

4

KWANZAA INTRODUCTION

In class today, Mrs. Mitchell read a non-fiction book about the African American holiday Kwanzaa. Annabelle hadn't realized how colorful this holiday was, or that it wasn't a religious holiday at all.

Kwanzaa is a holiday where African Americans reflect on and celebrate their African culture. The class found out that the holiday is celebrated for seven days, and on each day, a specific principle is highlighted and talked about. They also light a candle for each day on a candle holder called a Kinara.

Annabelle noticed that Kwanzaa was like Hanukkah because both holidays light a candle each day. However, a Hanukkah candle holder is called a Menorah, and it has white candles. The Kinara has three red candles on the left, three green candles on the right, and one black candle in the center.

Annabelle found it amazing that this holiday was founded in 1966 by an African Studies Professor named Dr. Maulana Karenga. Most of the holidays Annabelle was familiar with had been celebrated for many, many more years than Kwanzaa.

Mrs. Mitchell really wanted everyone to capture the heart of this holiday, so she had the class do a short research project. First, Mrs. Mitchell wrote each principle of Kwanzaa on an index card. Then she divided the class into seven groups and gave each one a card. Mrs. Mitchell wanted each group to represent their assigned principle in a unique way. They all brainstormed a list of ideas, which could include a poem, a song, a skit, a painting, or a dance. They tried to be as creative as they could.

"I don't believe I've ever had an assignment like this before in my life, but I definitely love it!" Annabelle began.

"I have no idea what on earth I could possibly do! Why can't she just give us a written assignment instead?" Jeanie asked, scratching her head.

"Because this is so much better and creative! This assignment is going to be so much fun!" Kaitlyn answered, happy they were doing a new project.

"I'm not good at dancing, so our project will have to be something written," Caleb mumbled.

"I love to dance and sing!" said

Victoria, who was always ready to showcase her own talents. "I wonder if we could do a combination of both!"

This assignment was creating much excitement in the classroom. Everyone was talking about it. Either they didn't like it at all, or they loved it. Mrs. Mitchell was hoping the project would get this kind of reaction. She couldn't wait to put the class in groups. But before she did, Mrs. Mitchell wanted to add a little more clarity to the assignment.

"It's very important that your group is in complete agreement as to what the whole group will do. Also, you can do a combination of one or two ideas, and it's very important that everyone do a part of the assignment. We will use the rest of the day to break into groups and start the planning process. Our Kwanzaa Celebration will take place on this Friday."

Mrs. Mitchell started to assign the students into working groups. Annabelle was grouped with Caleb and Jeanie. She had never been in a group with them before in the classroom, so she welcomed the opportunity. Even though she recalled Jeanie's negative comment about the project, she was still excited to work with her. So many ideas were going through Annabelle's mind at this time, but she was serious about not taking over the first group discussion with her partners.

When all the students met in their assigned groups for the first time, they excitedly talked about their projects. The first thing every group had to do was research their assigned principle and see what it meant. Then they had to explore all the different things they could do to represent the principle to the class.

Some of the discussions got extremely

loud, and Mrs. Mitchell had to go over and calm things down a bit.

Annabelle's group was really quiet at first, so she thought it was her duty to get the wheels turning on this assignment. "Our principle is Kujichagulia, which is pronounced koo-jee-chah-goo-LEE-ah, and that means self-determination," Annabelle explained.

Jeanie sunk back into her seat with a confused look on her face. "So what does that mean? This assignment is too hard. I knew I should have stayed home today." Jeanie groaned.

Caleb tried to bring order back to the group and get Jeanie under control. "Listen, you're going to have to get a grip on yourself. You're here now, so let's do some research!" Caleb took charge.

Annabelle was feeling pretty good about how Caleb took it upon himself to get involved. She had never seen that side of him before.

Annabelle Googled self-determination on her laptop and read the definition. "Self-determination means 'freedom to live as one chooses. To decide by yourself without listening to others.' So, I think it means that we should believe in ourselves and believe in our hopes and dreams," Annabelle said.

"Yeah, and maybe not be influenced by others in a negative way. Just know that you can do what you say you want to do," Caleb added.

"What does self-determination mean to you, Jeanie?" Annabelle asked.

"It means since I can't go home, I have to stay here and do this assignment no matter what," Jeanie said.

"Now that's the spirit, Jeanie!" Caleb encouraged her.

"So what kind of project could we do to bring this principle to life?" Annabelle asked, ready to write their ideas down with pencil and notepaper.

"I'm not good with song or dance, so maybe we could do a poem or something," Caleb suggested.

"Yeah, that sounds easy," Jeanie agreed, feeling relieved that there wouldn't be too much to do.

"So, a poem it is! We'll start tomorrow since class is almost over. Come with some good ideas tomorrow, and we'll get this done quickly," Annabelle said.

They all agreed as the bell rang to pack up for home.

5

NAME CHANGE

Annabelle couldn't stop thinking about her ideas for the Holiday Bash. She even thought of a new name for the event. Annabelle wasn't crazy about the word "bash" and was going to suggest another title for the event at the next meeting.

When the committee members gathered again, Mrs. Kessler appeared to have a slight smile on her face. Annabelle couldn't tell if it was a real smile or a fake one, but she welcomed it just as well.

Annabelle really wanted to convince Mrs. Kessler to be more open and positive about things concerning the holiday celebration. As Mrs. Jacobson hurried into the room last, the meeting finally began.

First, Mrs. Stewart recapped everything that was talked about at the last meeting.

"Okay, we have the basic outline of the event," she said. "Now I think we should break down the stations and assign two people to work on each one," said Mrs. Stewart.

Annabelle couldn't wait any longer to share her idea to rename the event, so she raised her hand and spoke up.

"Before we make assignments, I just wanted to ask if it might be possible to change the overall name of this event?" Annabelle asked, sounding confident.

"What name did you have in mind, Annabelle?" Mrs. Jacobson asked.

"I was thinking that we could call it 'The Super Holiday Spectacular!'" Annabelle said.

Both Mrs. Jacobson and Mrs. Stewart nodded their head in approval. Of course, Mrs. Kessler shook her head in disapproval.

"I personally like the title just the way it is. I see no reason in changing things around. Besides, the banner reads 'Holiday Bash' already," Mrs. Kessler said.

Annabelle's heart sank as she listened to Mrs. Kessler's words. She couldn't believe her idea was being shot down so quickly.

Mrs. Jacobson quickly spoke up, taking her side. "I think it's a great new name with substance and pizzazz!" she declared. "I personally love it!"

"And I love the title as well, Annabelle," Mrs. Stewart added. "I think a name change is just what we need to spice up this event a bit."

Kaitlyn, Barry, and Adele were all in favor of the name change as well.

"You know it will definitely be an added expense to print up yet another banner for this event. I really think we should try to keep our expenses down," Mrs. Kessler cautioned.

"I think we should put it to a vote. Everyone in favor of a new title for this event, raise your right hand," Mrs. Jacobson said.

Everyone in the room raised their hand except Mrs. Kessler.

"I guess we'll continue making arrangements for our Super Holiday Spectacular!" Mrs. Jacobson said with a grin. "And I just want you to know, Mrs. Kessler, that I definitely understand about the added cost for the new banner. So, I

will personally pay for the banner myself.
No worries!"

That announcement made Mrs.
Kessler feel a little better but not much.
She still hadn't put a real smile on her
face yet. The announcement also made
Annabelle feel much better as well. Just
knowing that everyone else loved her idea

about the name change really made up for the low feeling she had earlier from Mrs. Kessler's negative response.

Since Mrs. Jacobson celebrated Hanukkah every year, she volunteered to pair up with Kaitlyn to work on the Hanukkah station. She was already starting to envision all the materials she could bring from her house to represent Hanukkah.

Mrs. Stewart and Barry volunteered to work on the Christmas station. Barry thought that would be an easy station since he loved everything about Christmas. Adele and Annabelle were going to work on the Kwanzaa station. Since they were both studying about Kwanzaa in Social Studies, they thought it would be a perfect time to start thinking of some cool activities to do.

Mrs. Kessler really didn't volunteer for

any station, but she said she would oversee Annabelle and Adele since they didn't have an adult in their group.

Annabelle really couldn't imagine what the assistance from Mrs. Kessler was going to look like yet, but she was still set on convincing Mrs. Kessler to have a positive outlook on it. And if anyone could do that, it would certainly be Annabelle. She was hoping her charm, amazingly witty personality, and decision to never give up could win Mrs. Kessler over.

And so it was, the assignments were made. What would happen next, the committee could only imagine.

6

BRAINSTORMING
AND BONDING

At home, Annabelle was coming up with some great ideas for the Kwanzaa station for the Super Holiday Spectacular. Her family had celebrated Kwanzaa before, which made things a bit easier.

She invited her partner, Adele, over to help brainstorm some great ideas as well. Adele's family was from Nigeria, and she appreciated where she came from. Annabelle was quite surprised to learn that Adele and her family celebrated Kwanzaa too.

Annabelle was a people person and could get along with just about anyone. She had never worked with Adele before but was excited about this opportunity. Annabelle thought Adele was very respectful, neat, proper, and friendly. She always dressed in bright colors with cool designs on her clothes.

They both knew a little about the principles of Kwanzaa from what their parents taught them, but now they had to create some awesome activities for the students. They were both up for the challenge.

As Adele began sharing her first thoughts about Kwanzaa, the creative juices started to flow. "When my family celebrates Kwanzaa," she said, "the first thing we do is set up the Mkeka mat and set the Kinara, the candle holder, on it. Then we put the seven candles in the Kinara."

Just then a lightbulb went off in Annabelle's mind.

"That's it! The first activity can be creating our own Mkeka mat and Kinara with candles!" Annabelle said.

"That will definitely give them a good taste of Kwanzaa," Adele agreed.

"We can use card stock or cardboard so the Kinara can stand by itself. We can have all the pieces pre-cut to make it easy for everyone to put the Kinara together," Annabelle continued.

Getting excited now, Adele added, "We can also use red and green strips of card stock in a pattern to make the Mkeka mat by doing a paper weave. I think I may have a sample mat at home in our special Kwanzaa box that I can bring to school."

Annabelle nodded. "We'll definitely need to decorate the Kwanzaa station with red, black, and green colors. Maybe we could use streamers and balloons."

Writing down their ideas on a sheet of paper, Adele said, "I'm going to ask my mom if we can bring in some of our African art and sculptures to set on the

table so the people can see symbols of Africa all around."

"That's a great idea, Adele. Maybe we could borrow some books on African culture and Kwanzaa from the library to display."

"We may have to provide some handouts about Kwanzaa for the students to take with them because not that many people really know a lot about this holiday," Adele said, adding that item to her to-do list.

"You're right about that. I'm so glad Mrs. Mitchell is teaching us about it in our class. By the way, which Kwanzaa principle did your group get?" Annabelle asked.

"We got Kuumba (koo-OOM-bah), which means creativity, and that's what we're doing right now!" Adele said, laughing.

Both girls laughed and acted silly for a few minutes. Annabelle's mom brought them some juice and cookies so they could relax and have a little snack time. A break was definitely needed and appreciated.

Annabelle and Adele got to know each other a lot better during this time. They started talking about school, their hobbies, their family, and just about anything else that came up.

It's strange how a person can sit in a class with someone else for months and not really know him or her, even when that person is great. Annabelle began to think that it took bonding situations like this where they worked together to help them appreciate one another more.

The planning session went well. Annabelle and Adele clicked and connected with their creative ideas. They both realized how amazing and talented the other was. And they both were very excited about making their ideas come to life.

7

KWANZAA PROJECT

Today was the day for students to put the final touches on their Kwanzaa projects in Mrs. Mitchell's class and give their presentations.

Annabelle was impressed with the ideas Caleb brought to the table. He had started writing a poem, which was very good, and Annabelle ended up completing it with some ideas she had jotted down. Annabelle was very good at making up rhymes and catchy phrases about any topic.

When Jeanie finally arrived at the group meeting, she had quite the surprise. "Okay you two, I have something special up my sleeves," Jeanie said.

Annabelle and Caleb looked at each other, wondering what Jeanie had in mind.

"So what kind of surprise are you talking about, Jeanie?" Annabelle asked.

"I've been working on an African dance with these drum tracks!" Jeanie said with excitement.

Both Annabelle and Caleb gave confusing looks at Jeanie. They both thought to themselves, *How could this girl, who had no ideas before, now come up with an African dance?* They both wondered if she could really dance. Neither of them had ever seen Jeanie dance before.

They wondered if she were just going to be extremely silly and cause the group to look bad. Or maybe Jeanie was just holding back her greatness until this moment. They had to admit that her idea was really beyond what they had considered doing as a group. But Annabelle thought to herself, *What the heck, let's go with it. At the very least, it would be original.*

Every group only had fifteen minutes to finalize everything before it was time to present their Kwanzaa principle to the class. Mrs. Mitchell let some of the groups go outside in the hallway to prepare.

Jeanie played a musical drum track from her phone and started to show Caleb and Annabelle her dance. The routine was made up of a few simple steps that Jeanie repeated several times. It really wasn't too difficult, and Annabelle thought it was pretty good.

Caleb was trying to hold in his laughter. Annabelle gave Caleb the evil-eye and stepped on his foot so he wouldn't laugh at Jeanie. It was very obvious that Jeanie had spent a lot of time creating this dance for the presentation. Caleb definitely didn't appreciate the dance as much as Annabelle did.

Annabelle saw more than just the dance. She saw Jeanie's self-determination to perform this dance to the best of her ability. And that is just what this Kwanzaa principle was all about, Kujichagulia (koo-jee-chah-goo-LEE-ah), which means self-determination.

Mrs. Mitchell had a little surprise for her class as she called everyone together to start the presentations.

"I know I told everyone we'd be doing these presentations in our classroom, but our location has changed. We're actually going to do them on the stage in the auditorium since no one is using it at this time. So let's line up and walk to the auditorium quickly. We have seven presentations to get through," Mrs. Mitchell directed them.

The whole class was thrilled about the change in location and excited to stand on the stage and speak into the microphones. At least most of the class was excited. Jeanie and a few other students became a little nervous.

Annabelle noticed that Jeanie was staring into the distance with her eyes wide open.

"Jeanie, are you all right? You don't look like yourself. What's wrong?" Annabelle asked softly.

"I've never been on a stage before, and just the thought of dancing on stage is getting me nervous," Jeanie admitted.

Annabelle began to give her a pep talk. "Jeanie, just remember the meaning of our Kwanzaa principle, Kujichagulia (koo-jee-chah-goo-LEE-ah), which means self-determination. You've come so far. You worked so hard on this dance, and you were so determined to contribute to this presentation. You just have to believe in yourself. I know you can do it. Don't worry about who's looking at you because you're going to make us all very proud."

"Thank you, Annabelle. Maybe I could just close my eyes and go for it."

"Well, first you need to open your eyes to get on the stage," reminded Annabelle. "Maybe if you don't move around too much you could close your eyes for part of the dance. If you get too close to the edge of the stage, I'll have Barry look out for you," Annabelle offered.

"Deal!" Jeanie agreed.

When they got to the auditorium, all

the students sat down in the seats and waited until their Kwanzaa principle was called. Kaitlyn's group went first because they had the first principle of Kwanzaa, Umoja (oo-MOH-jah), which means unity.

Victoria and Jake were in Kaitlin's group. They did a short skit about sticking together as good friends. Most of it was done on the spot, but they really did a good job. The rest of the class gave them a lot of applause when they were finished.

Now it was time for Annabelle, Jeanie, and Caleb to present the second principle of Kwanzaa, Kujichagulia (koo-jee-chah-goo-LEE-ah). Jeanie slowly walked on to the stage and stared at everyone for a moment. Then she closed her eyes.

Caleb held up the sign with the Kwanzaa principle. Then he turned on

the drum track, using Jeanie's phone. Jeanie started dancing and opened her eyes a bit. Annabelle began reading the poem that went like this:

Kujichagulia—Self-Determination

We must make up our mind
to accomplish,
The goals we set forth for us.
Work on a plan.
Then take a stand.
These two things are a must.

If we are truly determined,
Then nothing will stop us for long.
We'll step through the mess,
Knowing it's a part of our test.
Indeed, God has made us strong.

Thank you.

As they finished, the class gave them loud applause. Jeanie sighed in relief that it was a success and gave them a big smile. All three of them held hands and took a group bow.

All the other presentations went extremely well, and Mrs. Mitchell was very pleased with everything. She had another surprise for the class, which was a Karamu feast to celebrate Kwanzaa. They didn't have any traditional foods, but Mrs. Mitchell did treat the class to a pizza Karamu feast! She also made special Zawadi gifts that were handmade Kwanzaa bookmarks and gave them out to everyone.

It's safe to say that the whole class learned a lot about Kwanzaa from doing this project, which turned out to be something that they would not soon forget.

8

CHRISTMAS LESSON

It was always a tradition in Mrs. Mitchell's class to read the story "'Twas the Night Before Christmas" during this time of the year. It didn't matter how old the students were, she just enjoyed sharing this particular story as an introduction to the Christmas holiday.

After the story, Mrs. Mitchell asked students to share some of their Christmas traditions with the class. Barry was the first to raise his hand.

"First, me and my brothers run into my parents' room and wake them up at about five o'clock in the morning so we can see what Santa brought us," Barry said.

Victoria, who was not impressed, weighed in on his Santa notion. "First of all, there is no Santa! Your mom and dad put all those presents under the tree," Victoria said with an attitude.

Barry had a confused and angry look on his face as he answered Victoria. "You don't know what you're talking about, Victoria! We have a fireplace and my dad always cleans it out the day before Christmas so Santa can come down the chimney with our presents!"

"I used to believe that when I was three years old, but then I grew up and my parents told me the truth. I guess some kids just haven't grown up yet," Victoria said and sighed.

Mrs. Mitchell noticed Barry becoming very upset and immediately jumped in.

"Different people believe different things and have different traditions. It doesn't make their way of thinking right or wrong; it's just what they believe right now. So, if that's part of Barry's tradition, then that's great. We're not going to shoot his belief down. And that's that!" Mrs. Mitchell said in a serious tone.

Kaitlyn raised her hand to share next. "When we all wake up on Christmas morning, Dad takes everyone out to breakfast. Then we come home and open our presents and play all day until our family comes over to eat with us for dinner. It's a really fun day!" Kaitlyn remembered.

"My family lets us open one present on Christmas Eve at night and then we go to a church service," Adele said.

"When we wake up in the morning," Annabelle said, "we all get dressed and go to the Children's Hope Charity in Lake Grove. My dad sits on the Board of Directors. We help serve breakfast to all the people and then give out gifts to everyone."

"That's really great, Annabelle. It's always a good thing to give to others who are less fortunate. It's so great to have different ways of enjoying and celebrating this holiday, isn't it class?" Mrs. Mitchell concluded.

"So how are we going to celebrate this holiday in our classroom?" Jake said.

"I'm so glad you asked, said Mrs. Mitchell. "First, we're all going to get with a partner and write a fiction story about Christmas. You can make it a mystery or a comedy or just something really silly. Then at the end of the day, everyone will pick a name of a student out of this bowl and you'll be their Secret Santa.

You'll be responsible for buying a special holiday gift for the classmate you choose. The gift should not cost more than ten dollars. And, you absolutely can't tell anyone the name you picked out of the bowl. It must be a secret."

The class became very excited about getting a holiday gift for a secret friend. But first they had to write a fiction story with a classmate and complete their assignment.

"Oh, and by the way, when you're writing your story with a friend," said Mrs. Mitchell as she revealed a list of words she hung up on the board, "you absolutely must include these holiday words: reindeer, Santa, candy canes, decorate, presents, stockings, chimney, sled, Christmas, and tree. I really want to challenge you to use these words in their proper context as you use your creativity."

Annabelle wondered who her partner would be. Mrs. Mitchell did things a little differently this time as she joined partners. She put all the boy's names in a bag and had each girl pull out a name from the bag to partner with. It's a good thing Mrs. Mitchell's class had an equal number of boys and girls so no one would be without a partner.

This was certainly a new way of organizing groups. The class had never drawn names from a bag before to get a partner. They were excited about the suspense of it all.

When it was Annabelle's time to draw from the bag, there were only two boys left, Dexter and Barry. Annabelle really hoped that she would pull Barry's name because they were already friends. Dexter, on the other hand, was very opinionated and blunt about things. They really didn't speak together that much.

When Annabelle looked at the folded paper from the paper bag, she tried to put a smile on her face, but it was definitely a fake smile to say the least. She had picked Dexter and wasn't very happy about it. But she knew that life goes on, and this pairing would be just another adventure.

Mrs. Mitchell gave the students twenty to thirty minutes to come up with a story. She instructed everyone to sit with their partner and get started right away since there wasn't much time.

Right away, Annabelle could see that she and Dexter were on completely different paths concerning the direction of this fiction story. Annabelle was thinking of writing a mystery, while Dexter was thinking of writing a silly comedy. Annabelle thought Dexter was silly most of the time in school already, so this should not have been a surprise to her at all.

Since Annabelle always wanted to keep the peace, she agreed to the silly story, but she didn't have very high expectations for the final product. Annabelle began by trying to include the holiday words into the story in their proper place, but that was not easy.

Annabelle soon realized that Dexter was very good at writing silly stories, although it wasn't really her thing. He was very direct, even in his silly writing. Annabelle just went with the flow of things and didn't rock the boat.

She knew the time for this writing assignment would be over quickly, and then this whole partnership would be history. Annabelle always prided herself in being able to get along with anyone, no matter how different they were, and this was definitely a situation that put her to the test.

After the story was completed, they smiled and went back to their own desks. Dexter even said that it was nice working with Annabelle. He had nothing negative to say about her. Annabelle took that as a well-deserved compliment.

Mrs. Mitchell said that everyone

would share their stories later in the week.

Now it was time to pick the mystery person for whom each student would buy a holiday gift. Annabelle picked Adele, and she immediately knew exactly what to get for her.

9

SECRET SANTA

All the students in Mrs. Mitchell's class were talking up a storm on the bus ride home. Everyone wanted to know who each person picked for their Secret Santa. It was really supposed to be a secret, and Annabelle treated it as such, even when Kaitlyn asked her the forbidden question.

"So, Annabelle, what name did you choose from the bowl for your Secret Santa?" Kaitlyn asked, eager to know.

Annabelle was upset by her friend's question. "I can't believe you're asking me that question, Kaitlyn," said Annabelle.

"You know Mrs. Mitchell instructed us not to tell anyone."

"But it's me, your best friend, Kaitlyn. Certainly, you can at least tell me," she pleaded.

"But what if I chose you? Then your gift wouldn't be a secret anymore because you would probably tell me what to get for you," Annabelle said.

"I guess you have a point there," replied Kaitlyn. "So you can get me whatever you want to, Annabelle. But you do know my favorite color is purple." Kaitlyn couldn't resist joking with her friend.

Annabelle laughed. "Whatever you say, Kaitlyn. Whatever you say."

That night Annabelle told her mom about what had happened in school and asked if they could go to the store to get the mystery gift for her classmate. Annabelle did share the name with her mom because she knew her mom wouldn't tell anyone, and she didn't go to school with her. Annabelle bought a really cool journal, a plume pen set, and some art supplies so she could personalize them for Adele.

The next couple of days were very hectic for Annabelle and the Super Holiday Spectacular Committee. Each group was putting finishing touches on the Holiday Station Activities.

A lot of the planning and preparation had to be done at home. Adele was coming over to Annabelle's house almost every day after school to help prepare the crafts.

Annabelle's mom helped out a lot too. It reminded Annabelle's mom of her elementary school days many years before. Annabelle and her mom were actually a lot alike. Her mom was smart as a whip and very active in school also. This is one of the reasons why her mom is so supportive of everything Annabelle does. Her mom marvels at her wit and capabilities for her age.

Finally, the end of the week came, and in Mrs. Mitchell's class it was time to share the Christmas fiction stories and reveal their Secret Santa. As each story was read, the class gave a good round of applause. There was also lots of laughter for the funny and silly stories.

When it was time for Annabelle and Dexter to share the story they wrote together, Dexter immediately took the lead and started reading the first half of the story. Annabelle noticed that his voice was very bright and clear. He used different voices to represent different characters.

When it was time for Annabelle to

read the second portion of the story, she tried to follow Dexter's lead and sound very clever as well. Annabelle was never one to be extremely silly, but somehow that funny side of her started to make itself known through her reading.

She found herself using a crazy voice that she had never used before. The class loved it and laughed along. Annabelle enjoyed it too.

Being goofy and silly was something she had never tried before. It's amazing how different personalities in people can challenge you to do things differently and explore and learn new things about yourself. That's exactly what Dexter did for Annabelle without even knowing it.

As a result, Annabelle got in touch with a different side of her personality. Annabelle concluded that when necessary, she was really good at being silly.

She didn't know if it was a good thing, or even something that she would do a lot, but at least she knew she could.

After the last story was read, everyone knew what was coming next and became very excited. Everyone's Secret Santa would finally be revealed!

Mrs. Mitchell asked them to get the gift they brought for their mystery person

and put it on their desk. Then one by one she motioned each student to give their mystery person their gift.

There was a lot of excitement and surprise. Then on the count of three, Mrs. Mitchell told everyone to open their gifts at the same time. Everyone was so excited.

Afterward, some of the girls hugged each other and the boys were giving high fives. This was a special moment to treasure forever.

10

SUPER HOLIDAY SPECTACULAR

When Annabelle woke up that day, she knew it was going to be one of the greatest days ever. At six thirty p.m. Melville School would be hosting their Annual Super Holiday Spectacular!

This is what the committee had worked on all month long, and today was the day. This was going to be a new and improved celebration with ideas from the mind of Annabelle Copeland.

Annabelle was very confident that things would go well, especially with a very supportive P.T.A. The parents started early in the morning putting up decorations.

When Annabelle arrived at school, she saw Mrs. Jacobson and some other parents hanging the new Super Holiday Spectacular sign above the Physical Education doors. All P.E. classes were going to be held in individual classrooms so the parents could start their major decorations early.

Annabelle and the other youth members of the committee could only help after school was over. During times like these, Annabelle wished she were an adult.

Annabelle's mom was at the school too since she was a P.T.A. member. She brought all the arts and crafts for the Kwanzaa station that Annabelle and Adele were going to run.

Adele's mom, Mrs. Benson, came too. She had a carload of African art, African sculptures, assorted pieces of African Kente cloth, and African culture books she had borrowed from the library.

Mrs. Copeland brought red, black, and green balloons and streamers. Together, Mrs. Benson and Mrs. Copeland were going to create a little African village for the Kwanzaa station.

Since it was the day before the holiday break, Mrs. Mitchell knew how excited the whole class was today. She also knew some of the students were very distracted by all the excitement happening in the school.

Three of her students had already left school early for the holiday break, so she took it easy on them work-wise. Mrs. Mitchell did Writing Workshop, Reading Workshop, Science review, and some holiday math sheets. They also did quiet reading and journal writing, and before they knew it, the day was almost over.

Annabelle and Adele didn't take the bus home today because their parents were already at the school. Kaitlyn and Barry didn't take the bus either because they were going to help decorate their stations in the gymnasium. When Annabelle, Adele, Kaitlyn, and Barry entered the gymnasium, they couldn't believe their eyes! The Hanukkah, Christmas, and Kwanzaa stations each looked amazing!

Another surprise they saw was Mrs. Kessler working right alongside the P.T.A. parents, hanging balloons and streamers. She had finally gotten into the holiday spirit after all.

Mrs. Kessler was wearing a Santa hat with bells and was humming a holiday song. That special sight was a holiday gift for the whole committee. Annabelle could tell that Mrs. Kessler's smile was real this time.

The parents had created a maze for the people to walk through as they appreciated all the unique artifacts. Everything

was hung on movable bulletin boards and chalkboards that were covered with festive paper. Annabelle thought that one of the parents must be an interior decorator and professional designer because of how creative and superior the displays looked.

Annabelle was so glad that the parents left the arts and crafts part to the youth. Doing arts and crafts was really Annabelle's specialty. So everyone went over to their station and started covering the tables with festive tablecloths and assembling all the crafts and games. This was the easy part of decorating and preparation.

There was another crew of parents working in the auditorium, creating the Winter Wonderland theme. White balloons and streamers were placed all around. The DJ was set up, playing cool music. The food tables were stocked and ready to go. Everything was coming together nicely, and they were having a good time.

At about five o'clock, everything was finished and looking spectacular. This event was really going to live up to its name, Super Holiday Spectacular! Everyone took a pizza and juice break for dinner. They probably wouldn't get another rest time for the whole night.

At exactly 6:30 p.m., the people came in like clockwork. A lot of "oohs" and "ahhs" were heard along with great reviews. No one had ever seen anything like this before at Melville School, or anywhere for that matter.

The committee had definitely outdone itself once again, and Annabelle was happy to be a part of such an awesome celebration.

ANNABELLE'S DISCUSSION CORNER

1. Which is your favorite December holiday and why?

2. List one thing that happens during each December holiday. Do some fun illustrations of each one.

3. How will you spend your special December holiday this year?

Don't forget to read the entire Amazing Annabelle Chapter Book Series!

*Please visit our website: amazingannabelle.com
for free teacher/student ELA resources to use in
your classroom or at home. Thank you!*

ABOUT THE AUTHOR

 Linda Taylor has been teaching students for over 25 years. She enjoys connecting with students on many levels. She is also the author of the *Daring David* series published by Lightswitch Learning. She also loves writing poetry. Linda lives on Long Island, New York.

ABOUT THE ILLUSTRATOR

 Kyle Horne has a B.A. in Visual Communications from S.U.N.Y. Old Westbury College in New York. Kyle has displayed his artwork in many local libraries. He lives on Long Island, New York.